TIMELESS SHAKESPEARE

TWELFTH NIGHT

William Shakespeare

– ADAPTED BY –

Emily Hutchinson

SADDLEBACK
EDUCATIONAL PUBLISHING

TIMELESS SHAKESPEARE

Hamlet

Julius Caesar

King Lear

Macbeth

The Merchant of Venice

A Midsummer Night's Dream

Othello

Romeo and Juliet

The Tempest

Twelfth Night

SADDLEBACK
EDUCATIONAL PUBLISHING
www.sdlback.com

© 2006, 2011 by Saddleback Educational Publishing

ISBN-13: 978-1-61651-111-1
ISBN-10: 1-61651-111-7
eBook: 978-1-60291-845-0

Printed in the United States of America
15 14 13 12 11   1 2 3 4 5

| Contents |

– BACKGROUND –

Orsino, Duke of Illyria, loves the Countess Olivia—but she will have nothing to do with him. Orsino sends his page Cesario (the disguised Viola, who has fallen in love with him) to plead his cause. Olivia falls in love with Cesario.

Viola's twin brother Sebastian (whom she believes has drowned in a shipwreck) arrives in Illyria. Olivia mistakes Sebastian for his disguised sister, and Sebastian falls in love with Olivia. More complications follow before identities are revealed and the story is brought to a happy end.

– CAST OF CHARACTERS –

ORSINO Duke of Illyria

SEBASTIAN a young gentleman, Viola's brother

ANTONIO a sea captain, friend of Sebastian

A SEA CAPTAIN friend of Viola

VALENTINE and **CURIO** gentlemen

SIR TOBY BELCH Olivia's uncle

SIR ANDREW AGUECHEEK Sir Toby's friend

OLIVIA a rich countess

VIOLA Sebastian's sister; later disguised as Cesario

MARIA Olivia's gentlewoman in waiting

MALVOLIO Olivia's steward

FABIAN Olivia's servant

FESTE Olivia's jester

LORDS, A PRIEST, SAILORS, OFFICERS, MUSICIANS, and **OTHERS**

ACT 1

| Scene 1 |

*An apartment in the duke's palace in Illyria. The **duke**, **Curio**, and **lords** enter. Musicians play.*

DUKE: If music be the food of love, play on,
Give me too much of it. By gorging,
The appetite may sicken and so die.
(Listening briefly) Enough! No more!
It's not as sweet now as it was before.
Oh, spirit of love! How alive and fresh
  you are!
In spite of being as deep as the sea,
Nothing precious comes to you without
Losing some of its value even in a minute!
Love has such variety that nothing can
Equal its extravagance.

CURIO: Will you go hunt, my lord?

DUKE: Hunt what, Curio?

CURIO: The hart.

DUKE *(placing his hand on his heart)*: Why,
That is what I'm doing. When my eyes first
Saw Olivia, I thought she purified the air.
That instant I was turned into a hart,
And my desires, like fierce and cruel hounds,
Have chased me ever since.

*(**Valentine** enters.)*

DUKE: Well? What news from her?

VALENTINE: My lord, I was not invited in.
Through her maid, the answer is this:
For seven summers, not even the sun
Will see her face. Like a nun, she will wear
A veil, weeping salt tears around her room,
To honor her dead brother's love, which
She wishes to keep fresh in sad memory.

DUKE: Oh, she who has such a tender heart
To pay this debt of love for a mere brother!
How will she love when Cupid's arrow
Strikes her heart?
Lead the way to sweet beds of flowers!
Love thoughts are richer under the bowers.

*(**All** exit.)*

| Scene 2 |

*The seacoast. **Viola, captain,** and **sailors** enter.*

VIOLA: What country is this, friends?

CAPTAIN: This is Illyria, lady.

VIOLA: What am I doing in Illyria?
My brother is in heaven. But maybe
He is not drowned. What do you think?

CAPTAIN: Luckily, you yourself were saved.

VIOLA: Oh, my poor brother!
Maybe he was saved, too.

CAPTAIN: True, madam. After our ship split,
When we were clinging to the drifting boat,
I saw your brother tie himself to a mast.
He was riding the waves
As long as I could keep him in sight.

VIOLA *(giving him money)*: For saying that,
Here's gold. My own escape gives me hope
That he escaped, too.
Do you know this country?

CAPTAIN: Yes. I was born and raised here.

VIOLA: Who governs here?

CAPTAIN: A noble duke named Orsino.

VIOLA: Orsino! My father spoke of him.
He was a bachelor then.

CAPTAIN: And he still is—or was till recently.
A month ago, when I left, I heard rumors
That he sought the love of fair Olivia.

VIOLA: Who's she?

CAPTAIN: A virtuous maiden, the daughter of
A count who died a year ago. He left her in
The protection of his son, her brother,
Who died soon after that. For his dear love,
They say, she has given up the company
And even sight of men!

VIOLA: I wish I served that lady and could

7

Stay out of the public eye until I found out
Better what my situation is!

CAPTAIN: That will not be easy. She will not
Consider any pleas—not even the duke's.

VIOLA: You seem like a good man, Captain.
Will you—I'll pay you well—help me
Disguise who I am? I want to serve this
duke.
You can present me as a young man to him.
It will be worth your trouble. I can sing, and
I can speak to him in many musical ways.
This will make me an attractive employee.
Whatever happens, time will tell.
Just be silent, will you? Well?

CAPTAIN: If silent I am unable to be,
Then may my eyes no longer see!

VIOLA: Thank you. *(She gestures.)* After you . . .

(They exit.)

| Scene 3 |

A room in Olivia's house. **Sir Toby Belch** *and* **Maria**
enter.

SIR TOBY: What the devil does my niece mean,
To take the death of her brother like this?
I'm sure worrying isn't good for her health.

MARIA: Really, Sir Toby, you must come home

earlier at night. Your niece does not like your late hours. Your drinking will be the end of you. I heard my lady talk of it yesterday. She also talked about a foolish knight that you brought here one night to be her wooer.

SIR TOBY: Who? Sir Andrew Aguecheek? He's the equal of any man in Illyria.

MARIA: What do you mean?

SIR TOBY: Why, he is rich!

MARIA: Perhaps. But his money will last only a year. He's a fool and a spendthrift.

SIR TOBY: Shame on you for saying so! He plays the violin, and he speaks three or four languages. He has all nature's finest gifts.

MARIA: He has indeed, like a natural born idiot! Besides being a fool, he likes to argue. Luckily, he also has the gift of cowardice. That slows down his zest in arguing. Without that, he would quickly have the gift of a grave—or so say those with brains!

SIR TOBY: They are scoundrels who say so! Who are they?

MARIA: The same who say he's drunk every night in your company.

SIR TOBY: With drinking to the health of my niece! What, my girl? Speak of the devil—here comes Sir Andrew Agueface.

(Sir Andrew Aguecheek *enters.)*

SIR ANDREW: Sir Toby Belch! Greetings!

SIR TOBY *(hugging him)***:** Sweet Sir Andrew!

SIR ANDREW *(to Maria)***:** Bless you, fair shrew. *(He thinks he's paid a compliment.)*

MARIA *(trying not to laugh)***:** And you too, sir.

SIR TOBY: Accost her, Sir Andrew. Accost her.

SIR ANDREW *(confused by a new word)***:** What does that mean?

SIR TOBY *(winking)***:** My niece's chambermaid!

SIR ANDREW *(misunderstanding)***:** Dear Miss Accost, I'd like to know you better.

MARIA: My name is Mary, sir.

SIR ANDREW: Dear Miss Mary Accost—

SIR TOBY *(interrupting)***:** You've got it wrong, knight. "Accost" means to make advances, take her on, flirt with her, attack her.

SIR ANDREW: My word, I wouldn't tackle her in this company. Is *that* what the word means?

MARIA *(turning to go)***:** Goodbye, gentlemen.

(Maria *exits.)*

SIR TOBY: Oh, knight! You need a glass of wine. When have I ever seen you so put down? Why, my dear knight?

SIR ANDREW: Sir Toby, your niece will not see me. Even if she did, it's four to one she'd have nothing to do with me. The count himself, who lives near here, is wooing her.

SIR TOBY: She'll have nothing to do with the count. She won't marry above herself—either in fortune, age, or intelligence. I have heard her swear it. Nonsense! You stand a good chance with her, man!

SIR ANDREW: I'll stay a month longer. After all, I'm a fellow with a playful mind. I love costume parties and dances, sometimes both together.

SIR TOBY: Are you good at dancing, knight?

SIR ANDREW: As good as any man in Illyria, provided he's my inferior. But I can't compare with an experienced man.

SIR TOBY: How good are you at a reel, knight?

SIR ANDREW: Well, I think I can dance as neatly as any man! *(He demonstrates, poorly.)*

SIR TOBY *(pretending to admire him)*: Why have you been hiding all your talent? Why have these gifts been kept behind a curtain? They are likely to get dusty, like a painting. Why don't you dance the reel on your way to church and come home doing a fling? If I were you, my very walk would be a jig. What are you

11

thinking? Is this the kind of world to hide virtues in? Looking at the excellent shape of your leg, I'd say it was formed under the influence of a dancing star.

SIR ANDREW *(boasting)*: Yes, it is strong—and it does look good in a flame-colored stocking. Shall we do some reveling?

SIR TOBY: Of course! Let me see you dance. *(Sir Andrew begins to dance.)* Higher!
(Sir Andrew does his best.) Ha, ha! Excellent!

*(**They** exit.)*

| Scene 4 |

*A room in the duke's palace. **Valentine** enters with **Viola**, who is dressed as a young man and now known as Cesario.*

VALENTINE: If the duke continues to favor you, Cesario, you are likely to be promoted soon. He has known you only three days, and already you are no stranger.

VIOLA: Thank you. Here comes the duke now.

*(The **duke, Curio**, and **attendants** enter.)*

DUKE: Has anyone seen Cesario?

VIOLA: Ready to serve you, my lord.

DUKE *(to his attendants)*: Stand aside a moment.
  (to Viola) Cesario, you know everything.
  I have opened my secret soul to you.
  Therefore, young man, go to her.
  Stand at her doors, and tell them that
    your foot
  Will take root until you're asked to come in.

VIOLA: Surely, my noble lord,
  If she is as lost in her sorrow as they say,
  She will never let me in.

DUKE: Do not take no for an answer!

VIOLA: Suppose I do speak with her, my lord.
  What then?

DUKE: Oh, tell her of the passion of my love.
  Surprise her with talk of my deep devotion.
  It will be good for you to speak to her.
  She will listen better to a youth
  Than to an older messenger.

VIOLA: I do not think so, my lord.

DUKE: Dear boy, believe it.
  You are perfect for this affair.
  Do well in this, and I will reward you with
  A share of my fortune.

VIOLA: I'll do my best to woo your lady.
  (Aside) A difficult job! Whomever I woo,
  What I really want is to marry *you!*

| Scene 5 |

A room in Olivia's house. **Maria** *and* **Feste** *enter.*

MARIA: Either tell me where you have been, or I will not open my mouth to make any excuses for you. My lady will fire you for being gone so long.

FESTE: Well, let her! At least it's summer, so I won't freeze.

MARIA: Here comes my lady now. You'd better be thinking of a good excuse.

*(**Maria** exits.)*

FESTE *(as if in prayer)*: Oh, Wit, if you please, help me be witty. Jesters who think they're witty often prove to be fools. Since I know I'm not witty, I may pass for a wise man. What's the old saying? "Better a witty fool than a foolish wit."

*(**Olivia** and **Malvolio** enter, followed by **attendants**.)*

God bless you, lady!

OLIVIA *(with a weary gesture)*: Take the fool away.

FESTE *(to the attendants)*: Didn't you hear her, fellows? Take the lady away!

OLIVIA: Don't talk nonsense. You have a dry wit. I've had enough of you. Besides, you're becoming dishonest.

FESTE: Two faults, madam, that drink and good advice will cure. Give the dry fool drink, and soon the fool is not dry. Tell the dishonest man to mend himself, and if he does, he is no longer dishonest. If he cannot mend himself, let a cheap tailor mend him. Anything that is mended is patched. Virtue that goes wrong is patched with sin. Sin that mends its ways is patched with virtue. If this simple logic works for you, fine. If not, what can be done about it? *(to attendants)* The lady said to take away the fool. Therefore, I say again, take her away.

OLIVIA: Sir, I told them to take *you* away.

FESTE: An error in the highest degree! Lady, "the hood doesn't make the monk." In other words, don't be deceived by my jester's clothing. Good lady, allow me to prove that you are a fool.

OLIVIA: Can you do it?

FESTE: Easily, good lady.

OLIVIA: Make your proof.

FESTE: I must ask you questions to do it, madam.

OLIVIA: Well, sir, for lack of anything better to do, I'll go along with you.

FESTE: My lady, why are you in mourning?

OLIVIA: Good fool, for my brother's death.

FESTE: I think his soul is in hell, my lady.

OLIVIA: I know his soul is in heaven, fool.

FESTE: The more fool you are, my lady, to mourn for your brother's soul being in heaven. *(to attendants)* Take away the fool, gentlemen.

OLIVIA *(to Malvolio)*: What do you think of this fool, Malvolio? Isn't he improving?

MALVOLIO: Yes, and he'll continue to do so, till he's in his death throes. Old age, which decays the wise, always makes fools even more foolish.

FESTE: May God send you, sir, a speedy old age, to increase your folly even more! Sir Toby will swear that I am no great wit, but he wouldn't take two cents to swear that you are not a fool.

OLIVIA: What do you say to that, Malvolio?

MALVOLIO: I am amazed that your ladyship takes delight in such an empty-headed rascal.

OLIVIA: Oh, you take yourself too seriously, and your judgment is poor. A kind person overlooks the faults in others.

(Maria returns.)

MARIA: Madam, there is at the gate a young gentleman who wishes to speak with you.

OLIVIA: From the Count Orsino, is he?

MARIA: I don't know, madam. He's a fair young man, with several attendants.

OLIVIA: Who of my people is keeping him waiting?

MARIA: Sir Toby, madam, your relative.

OLIVIA: Fetch Sir Toby away, please. He talks like a madman. Shame on him!

(Maria exits.)

You go, Malvolio. If he has a message from the count, tell him I am sick, or not at home, or say whatever you wish to get rid of him.

(Malvolio exits. Olivia turns to Feste.)

Now you see, sir, how people dislike your fooling.

FESTE: You have spoken for us jesters, madam, as if your eldest son were a fool. May God cram his skull with brains—because here comes one of your relatives who is not too bright.

(Sir Toby Belch enters.)

OLIVIA: Upon my honor, he's half drunk! *(to Sir Toby)* What kind of person is at the gate, cousin?

SIR TOBY: A gentleman.

OLIVIA: A gentleman? What gentleman?

17

SIR TOBY: There's a gentleman here.
  (He belches loudly.) Blame these pickled
    herrings!
  (to Feste) Greetings, fool!

FESTE: Dear Sir Toby!

OLIVIA: Cousin, cousin, how do you come to
    have this dullness, this lethargy, so early?

SIR TOBY *(misunderstanding)***:** Lechery! I defy
    lechery. There's someone at the gate.

OLIVIA: Yes, indeed. What sort of man is he?

SIR TOBY: Let him be the devil if he wishes, I
    don't care. It's all the same to me.

*(**Sir Toby** exits.)*

OLIVIA: What's a drunken man like, fool?

FESTE: Like a drowning man, a fool, and a
    madman. One drink too many makes
    him foolish, the second makes him mad,
    and the third drowns him.

OLIVIA: Go and find the coroner. Let him
    take my cousin, for he's in the third
    degree of drink. He's drowned.
    Go and look after him.

FESTE: He's only at the mad stage, madam.
    The fool will look after the madman.

*(**Feste** exits. **Malvolio** returns.)*

MALVOLIO: Madam, the young fellow at the

door swears he will speak with you. I told him you were sick. He said he already knew that, and for that reason has come to speak with you. I told him you were asleep. He claims to already know that, too, and for that reason comes to speak to you. What can I say to him, lady? He has an answer for everything.

OLIVIA: Tell him that he shall not speak with me.

MALVOLIO: He has been told so. He says he'll stand at your door like a flagpole, or prop up a bench—but he will speak to you.

OLIVIA: What kind of man is he?

MALVOLIO: Why, of the human race . . .

OLIVIA: What type of man?

MALVOLIO: Very rude. He'll speak to you, whether you wish it or not.

OLIVIA: What's he like, and how old is he?

MALVOLIO: Not old enough to be a man, nor young enough to be a boy. He is very good-looking.

OLIVIA: Let him come in. Call my gentlewoman.

MALVOLIO: Gentlewoman! My lady calls.

*(**Malvolio** exits. **Maria** returns.)*

OLIVIA: Give me my veil. Throw it over my face.

We'll hear Orsino's message once again.

*(**Viola**, dressed as **Cesario**, enters.)*

VIOLA: The lady of the house, which is she?

OLIVIA: I'll answer for her. What is it?

VIOLA *(beginning her prepared speech)*: Most radiant, exquisite, and unmatched beauty . . . *(breaking off)* Please, tell me if this is the lady of the house, for I never saw her. I'd hate to waste my speech. Apart from the fact that it is very well-written, I have worked hard to learn it by heart. *(Maria cannot keep from laughing.)* Please, do not laugh at me. I am very sensitive.

OLIVIA: Where have you come from, sir?

VIOLA: I can say little more than what I've learned, and that question isn't in my script. Gentle madam, give me some small assurance that you are the lady of the house.

OLIVIA: Are you an actor?

VIOLA: No. And yet, I swear that I am not what I appear to be. Are you the lady of the house?

OLIVIA: I am.

VIOLA: Then I will go on with my speech in your praise. After that, I will get to the heart of my message.

OLIVIA: Get to the point. Forget the praise.

VIOLA: I worked hard to learn it, and it's poetic.

OLIVIA: It's all the more likely to be fake. I beg you to keep it to yourself. I heard you were brazen at my gates. I allowed you to come in, more to wonder at you than to hear you. If you're mad, be gone. If you're sane, be brief. I'm not in the mood to have such a silly conversation. Say what's on your mind.

VIOLA: I am a messenger.

OLIVIA: Surely, you must have some hideous message to deliver, when the formalities are so complicated. What is it?

VIOLA: It is for your ears alone. I bring you no declaration of war, no demands for taxes. I hold an olive branch in my hand. My words are full of peace, not argument.

OLIVIA: Yet you began rudely. What are you? What do you want?

VIOLA: I was rude because I was treated rudely. What I am and what I want are as secret as virginity. To your ears, divine; To any other's, profane.

OLIVIA *(to Maria)***:** Leave us alone. I'll hear this "divinity."

(Maria exits.)

VIOLA: Most sweet lady . . .

OLIVIA: Where does your text come from?

VIOLA: Orsino's heart.

OLIVIA: His heart? In what chapter of his heart?

VIOLA: To answer in the same style: Chapter One of his heart.

OLIVIA: Oh, I have already read it. It is heresy. Have you anything else to say?

VIOLA: Good madam, let me see your face.

OLIVIA: Has your master told you to negotiate with my face? Well, we will draw the curtain and show you the picture. *(She lifts her veil.)* Isn't it a good likeness?

VIOLA: Excellently done, if it's all God's work.

OLIVIA: It is protected, sir. It will endure wind and weather.

VIOLA: It is beauty well-blended. The colors
Were done by Nature's own sweet hand.
Lady, you are the cruelest woman alive,
If you will take these gifts to the grave,
And leave the world no copy.

OLIVIA: Oh, sir, I will not be so hard-hearted.
I'll publish various lists of my beauty.
It will be inventoried, and every detail
Labeled as I wish. Item: two lips, fairly red.
Item: two gray eyes with lids to them.
Item: one neck, one chin, and so forth.
Were you sent here to praise me?

22

VIOLA: I see what you are!
　　You are too proud. But, even if you are
　　The devil, you are beautiful!
　　My lord and master loves you.

OLIVIA: How does he love me?

VIOLA: With great adoration and many tears.
　　With groans that thunder out their love.
　　With sighs of fire.

OLIVIA: Your lord knows my feelings.
　　I cannot love him. But I believe he is
　　　　virtuous. I know he is noble, wealthy,
　　　　and youthful.
　　He is well-regarded, free-spirited, educated,
　　　　and brave. He is also said to be gracious.
　　Yet I cannot love him.
　　He should have accepted my answer long ago.

VIOLA: If I loved you as my master does,
　　With such suffering and agony,
　　I would find no sense in your answer.
　　I would not understand it.

OLIVIA: Why, what would you do?

VIOLA: I'd make myself a cabin at your gate,
　　And call upon my loved one in the house.
　　I'd write devoted songs of hopeless love,
　　And sing them loud, even in the dead of
　　　　night.
　　I'd shout your name to the echoing hills,
　　And make the echoes on the air

23

Cry out "Olivia!" Oh, you couldn't live
On this earth without feeling pity for me.

OLIVIA: In your case, you might succeed.
What is your background?

VIOLA: Better than my present situation.
I am a gentleman.

OLIVIA: Go back to your lord. I cannot love
him. Tell him to send no more
messages—
Unless, by chance, you come to me again
To tell me how he takes it. Goodbye.
I thank you for the trouble you have taken.
(She hands Viola some money.) Spend this for me.

VIOLA *(refusing)***:** I am no paid messenger, lady.
Keep your money. It is my master,
Not myself, who lacks reward.
May the man you love have a heart of stone,
And let your passion, like my master's,
Be treated with contempt!
Farewell, you cruel beauty!

(Viola exits.)

OLIVIA: What is your background?
"Better than my present situation.
I am a gentleman."
I'll swear an oath you are!
Your voice, face, limbs, action, and spirit
Indicate a five-star pedigree. *(She thinks.)*

Not too fast . . . softly, softly! Now if the
  master were the man . . . what then?
Can one fall in love so fast?
I think I feel this youth's perfections
Creeping their way in through my eyes.
Well, let it be. *(She calls out.)* Hello there!
Malvolio! *(She takes a ring off her finger.)*

*(**Malvolio** returns.)*

MALVOLIO: Here, madam, at your service.

OLIVIA *(handing him the ring)*: Run after that
Rude messenger fellow, the count's man.
He left this ring behind him,
Whether I wanted it or not.
Tell him I won't have it!
Tell him not to mince words with his lord
Nor give him false hopes. I am not for him.
If the youth will come this way tomorrow,
I'll give him my reasons. Hurry, Malvolio!

MALVOLIO: Madam, I will.

*(**Malvolio** exits.)*

OLIVIA: I don't know what I'm doing!
I'm afraid my eyes may be fooling me.
Fate, show your power.
We do not control our own destiny.
What must be, must be!

*(**Olivia** exits.)*

ACT 2

| Scene 1 |

The seacoast. ***Antonio*** *and* ***Sebastian*** *enter.*

ANTONIO: Can't I go with you?

SEBASTIAN: Forgive me, no. I've had bad luck lately. My bad luck might affect yours. Let me bear my troubles alone.

ANTONIO: Tell me where you are going.

SEBASTIAN: No, really, sir. My planned trip is nothing but wandering. I see that you are too polite to insist on information that I wish to keep to myself. But good manners require me to tell you that Sebastian is my real name, though I said it was Roderigo. My father was Sebastian of Messaline, who died and left me and my twin sister behind. We were born within the same hour. If the heavens had wished it, we would have died the same way! But you, sir, changed that. About an hour or so before you rescued me from the sea, my sister drowned.

ANTONIO: How terrible!

SEBASTIAN: Even though she looked like me, many people thought she was beautiful.

I will say this about her: She had a beautiful
mind. Now she is drowned, sir, in saltwater.
(He chokes back a tear.) I seem to drown her
memory in salty tears.

ANTONIO *(realizing Sebastian is a gentleman)***:**
Pardon me, sir, for my humble hospitality.

SEBASTIAN: Oh, good Antonio, forgive me for
being so much trouble.

ANTONIO: If you don't want me to die for my
love, let me be your servant.

SEBASTIAN: Unless you want to undo what you
have done—that is, kill the man you
have just rescued—don't ask that. For
now, goodbye. My heart has such tender
feelings for you, the least thing might
make me cry. I am going to the court of
Count Orsino. Farewell.

*(**Sebastian** exits.)*

ANTONIO: May the gods go with you!
I have many enemies in Orsino's court,
Or else I would follow you there.
(He turns to go, and then stops to think again.)
But come what may, I am so fond of you
That danger seems like fun—so I will go!

*(**Antonio** exits.)*

| Scene 2 |

*The street. **Viola** and **Malvolio** enter.*

MALVOLIO: Weren't you with the Countess Olivia just now? *(offering a ring)* She returns this ring to you, sir. You might have saved me trouble by taking it away yourself. Please assure your lord that she wants nothing to do with him. And one more thing: You must never be so bold as to come again on his affairs—unless it is to report how he takes this. *(throwing the ring on the ground)* Take it back.

VIOLA *(stopping to think, and then realizing the situation)***:** I don't want the ring back.

MALVOLIO: Sir, you rudely threw it to her, and she wants me to return it the same way. If it is worth stooping for, there it is where you can see it. If not, let it belong to whoever finds it.

(Malvolio exits.)

VIOLA: I gave her no ring. What does she mean? Heaven forbid that my looks charmed her! She looked me over so closely that I thought her eyes had tied her tongue. She loves me, that's sure. Her passion Invites me through this rude messenger. *(scornfully)* She won't have my lord's ring!

Why, he didn't send her one!
If it's true that I'm the man she loves,
Poor lady, she'd be better off loving a dream.
My disguise is a form of wickedness
That helps the devil do his work.
How easy it is for attractive but false men
To work their way into women's hearts!
Alas, our weakness is the cause, not we.
What we are made of, that we must be.
(She thinks.) How will this turn out?
My master loves her dearly,
And I, poor devil, am just as fond of him.
Not knowing, she seems to dote on him.
What will become of this? As a man,
I have no chance of my master's love.
Oh time, you must untangle this, not I.
It is too hard a knot for me to untie!

*(**Viola** exits.)*

| Scene 3 |

*A room in Olivia's house. **Sir Toby Belch** and
Sir Andrew Aguecheek enter. They are both drunk.*

SIR TOBY: Come on, Sir Andrew. Not to be in
bed after midnight is to be up early. You
know that.

SIR ANDREW: No, upon my word, I do not
know that. To be up late is to be up late.

29

SIR TOBY: That's false logic. I hate it as I hate an unfilled glass! To be up after midnight, and to go to bed then is early. Aren't our lives made up of the four elements of fire, water, air, and earth?

SIR ANDREW: So they say. But I think it really consists of eating and drinking.

SIR TOBY: You are a scholar! Let us therefore eat and drink. *(Calling)* Maria, I say! Some wine!

*(**Feste** enters.)*

FESTE: How goes it, my friends?

SIR TOBY: Welcome, fool. Now let's have a song.

SIR ANDREW: Upon my word, the fool has an excellent voice. *(to Feste)* You were in rare form last night! The entertainment was very good. Here's some money. Let's have a song.

FESTE: Would you like a love song, or a song about how good life is?

SIR TOBY: A love song, a love song.

FESTE *(singing as he plays his lute)***:** Oh, mistress mine, where are you roaming?
Oh, stay and hear. Your true love's coming,
Who can sing both high and low.
Go no further, pretty sweeting;
Journeys end in lovers meeting,

Every wise man's son does know.

SIR ANDREW: Extremely good, indeed!

SIR TOBY: Good, good.

FESTE *(singing)***:** What is love? It's not hereafter.
Present mirth has present laughter.
What's to come is still unsure.
In delay there lies no plenty.
Then come kiss me, sweet and twenty.
Youth's a stuff will not endure!

SIR ANDREW: A sweet voice, as I am a true
knight.

SIR TOBY: Shall we sing a song together?

SIR ANDREW: If you love me, let's do it.

31

SIR ANDREW: Let's sing "You knave." You start, fool. It begins, "Hold your peace."

FESTE: I shall never begin if I hold my peace.

SIR ANDREW: That's good! Come on, let's begin.

*(They sing. **Maria** enters.)*

MARIA: What a racket you're making! If my lady hasn't told her steward Malvolio to throw you out, don't ever trust me again.

SIR TOBY: My lady's a prude. Malvolio
Is an old woman, and—
(singing) Three merry men we be!
Tilly-valley, lady.

FESTE: I swear, the knight's in rare form.

SIR ANDREW: Yes, he does well enough if he's in the mood. And so do I. He does it with better style, but I do it more naturally.

SIR TOBY *(singing)***:** Oh, the twelfth day of December—

MARIA: For the love of God, *quiet!*

*(**Malvolio** enters.)*

MALVOLIO: Gentlemen, are you mad, or what?
Have you no sense or good manners?
To raise such a squawking ruckus
Makes an alehouse of my lady's home.
Have you no respect?
Sir Toby, I must be straight with you.

My lady welcomes you as her kinsman,
But she doesn't like your bad behavior.
Stay if you can behave yourself. If not—
And if it would please you to leave—she
Is very willing to see you go.

SIR TOBY: Are you any more than a steward?
Just because *you* are virtuous,
Must we be, too?

FESTE: Yes, by Saint Anne! The fun is over!

SIR TOBY: Is it really? Go, sir, polish the
leash my lady keeps around your neck.
(calling) More wine, Maria!

MALVOLIO: Miss Mary, if you valued my lady's
good opinion, you would not supply the
drink for this rude behavior. *(shaking his
fist)* She shall know of it, by this hand.

(Malvolio exits.)

MARIA: Go shake your ears, you donkey!

SIR ANDREW: That's as good as making a fool of
a man by not showing up for a duel!

SIR TOBY: Challenge Malvolio, sir knight!
I'll deliver it to him in person!

MARIA: Sweet Sir Toby, be patient for tonight.
Since the count's young man visited my
Lady today, she's been very touchy.
Leave Malvolio to me! I can make him
Into a byword for stupidity.

33

SIR TOBY: Tell us how! Tell us how!

MARIA: He thinks he's so full of excellence that Everyone who sees him must love him. That weakness will be his downfall.

SIR TOBY: What will you do?

MARIA: I will drop some love letters in his path. The letters will lovingly describe the color of his beard, the shape of his leg, the way he walks, and the expression in his eyes. I can write just like my lady. Sometimes we cannot even remember who wrote what.

SIR TOBY: Excellent! I smell a rat.

SIR ANDREW: I smell it, too.

SIR TOBY: He will think the letters come from My niece, who must be in love with him.

MARIA: I am betting on a horse of that color. I am sure of it.

SIR ANDREW: Oh, yes, it will be admirable!

MARIA: Royal sport, I guarantee you. I know my medicine will work with him. You two, along with Fabian, can hide where he will find the letter. Then watch him interpret it. But for tonight: to bed, and farewell.

(*Maria* exits.)

SIR ANDREW: Believe me, she's a good one!

SIR TOBY: And she adores me. What do you
   think of that?

SIR ANDREW: I was adored once, too.

SIR TOBY: I'll go heat some sherry. It's too late to
   go to bed now. Come on, knight!

*(**Sir Toby** and **Sir Andrew** exit.)*

| Scene 4 |

*A room in the duke's palace. The **duke**, **Viola**, **Curio**,
and **others** enter.*

DUKE: Good morning! Let's have music.
   (to Viola) Please, good Cesario, sing
   That quaint, old song we heard last night.
   Come, just one verse.

CURIO: If it pleases your lordship, the one
   who should sing it is Feste, the jester.
   He's around the house somewhere.

DUKE: Seek him out, and play the tune
   meanwhile. *(**Curio** exits. Music plays.)*
   (to Viola) Come here, boy.
   If you ever fall in love,
   In the sweet pangs of it, remember me:
   For all true lovers act just as I do—
   Unstable and fickle in everything but
   Their obsession with the creature who is
   loved. How do you like this tune?

35

VIOLA: It gives an exact echo of the throne
Where love sits.

DUKE: You speak like an expert!
I'd bet that, even though you are young,
You have your eye on someone you love.
Isn't that so, boy?

VIOLA: A little—if I may say so.

DUKE: What kind of woman is she?

VIOLA: She looks like you.

DUKE: She is not worth you, then.
How old is she?

VIOLA: About as old as you, my lord.

DUKE: Too old, by heaven! The woman
Should always marry someone older,
So she can adjust herself to suit him.
Then she will always keep a steady place
In her husband's heart.
For, boy, no matter how we flatter ourselves,
Men's affections are unstable,
Full of desire and fickle—
Sooner lost and won, than women's are!

VIOLA: I think you are right, my lord.

DUKE: Then let your love be younger than you,
Or your affection will not last.
For women are like roses, fair flowers
Once displayed, that fade that very hour.

VIOLA: And so they are. Alas, that it is so,
To die, just as they to perfection grow!

*(**Curio** and **Feste** enter again.)*

DUKE: Oh, fellow, come on—
  The song you sang last night.

FESTE: Are you ready, sir?

DUKE: Yes. Please sing.

FESTE *(singing along to the music)*: Come away,
    come away, death.
  And in sad cypress let me be laid.
  Fly away, fly away, breath.
  I am slain by a fair cruel maid.
  My shroud of white, stuck all with yew,
  Oh, prepare it!

DUKE *(giving him money)*: For your pains.

FESTE: No pains, sir. I take pleasure in singing.

DUKE: I'll pay for your pleasure, then.

FESTE: True, sir. Pleasure must be paid for at
    one time or another.

DUKE: That's enough of that!

FESTE: May the gods protect you. Farewell.

*(**Feste** exits.)*

DUKE: The rest of you may leave.

*(**Curio** and **attendants** exit.)*

DUKE: *(to Viola)* Once more, Cesario,
  Go to that same cruel lady.
  Tell her my noble love puts no value on large
    estates of dirty land. Tell her that

What attracts my soul to her is her beauty,
In which she's a miracle and a queen of gems.

VIOLA: But what if she cannot love you, sir?

DUKE: I do not accept that answer.

VIOLA: Truly, but you must. Suppose that
  some lady—as perhaps there is—
Loves you as much as you love Olivia.
You cannot love her, and tell her so.
Mustn't she then accept your answer?

DUKE: No woman's heart can bear so strong
A passion as love gives my heart.
No woman's heart is big enough for it!
Women lack staying power.
Alas, their love may be called appetite.
It's not driven by emotion but by taste.
But my appetite is as hungry as the sea
And can digest as much. Do not compare
The love a woman can have for me
With the love I have for Olivia.

VIOLA: Yes, but I know— *(She breaks off, afraid to
  reveal herself.)*

DUKE: What do you know?

VIOLA: How well women may love men.
In fact, they are as true of heart as we.
My father had a daughter who loved a man—
As I might—if I were a woman—
Love your lordship.

DUKE: And what's her story?

VIOLA: A blank, my lord.
She never revealed her love,
But let her secret, like a worm in the bud,
Feed on her rosy cheek. She pined in thought,
And sickened with grief. Wasn't this love?
We men say more and swear more, but indeed
Our behaviors are not sincere.
We tend to vow a lot, but love little.

DUKE: But did your sister die of her love, my boy?

VIOLA: I am all the daughters that my father has,
And all the brothers, too—
But I may be wrong about that.
(She's still hoping that Sebastian didn't drown.)
Sir, shall I go to this lady?

DUKE: Yes, that's the idea. *(giving Viola a jewel)*
Go to her quickly. Give her this jewel.
Say that my love cannot be denied.

*(**Duke** and **Viola** exit.)*

| Scene 5 |

*Olivia's garden. **Sir Toby Belch, Sir Andrew Aguecheek,** and **Fabian** enter.*

SIR TOBY: Come along, Mister Fabian.

FABIAN: I'm coming. If I miss a minute of this sport, may I be boiled to death in misery!

SIR TOBY: Won't you be glad to see the mean, rascally dog come to great shame?

FABIAN: I will rejoice, man!

(Maria enters.)

SIR TOBY: Here comes the little villain! How are things, my golden one?

MARIA: All three of you, hide behind the hedge.
Malvolio's coming! He's been in the sun,
Practicing bows to his own shadow.
For the love of mockery, watch him!
This letter will make an idiot of him.
Hide, in the name of practical joking!

*(The men hide themselves as **Maria** throws down a letter. Then she exits and **Malvolio** enters.)*

MALVOLIO: Everything is just a matter of luck.
Maria once said that Olivia liked me.
I've heard hint that if she ever loved
anyone, it would be someone like me.
Besides, she treats me with more
respect than any of the others.
What should I think about that?

SIR TOBY: What a conceited rogue!

FABIAN: *Shhh!* Thinking makes him a rare
peacock. Look how he struts under his
raised feathers!
Now he's deeply in thought.
Imagination is swelling his head.

MALVOLIO: I can see myself sitting in my chair of state—

SIR TOBY *(angrily)*: Oh, if I only had a stone to hit him in the eye!

MALVOLIO: —calling my servants to me, in my fancy velvet gown, having come from a daybed, where I've left Olivia sleeping—

SIR TOBY *(more angrily)*: Fire and brimstone!

FABIAN: Oh, quiet, quiet.

MALVOLIO: —I'd send for my kinsman Toby.

SIR TOBY *(even more angrily)*: Bolts and shackles!

FABIAN: Oh, quiet, quiet!

MALVOLIO: Seven of my people obediently go to get him. I frown meanwhile, maybe wind up my watch or play with some rich jewel. Toby comes and bows to me.

SIR TOBY *(totally outraged by now)*: Shall this fellow be allowed to live?

FABIAN: Even if wild horses tried to drag words out of us, be silent now!

MALVOLIO: I extend my hand to him like this *(he stretches forth a limp hand)*, holding back my familiar smile with a look of authority—

SIR TOBY: And doesn't Toby hit you in the mouth then?

MALVOLIO: —saying, "Cousin Toby, since good

41

fortune has given me your niece, I have the right to say this."

SIR TOBY: What? What?

MALVOLIO: "You must stop your drunkenness."

SIR TOBY: Away, you scab!

FABIAN: Be patient, or we'll give our game away.

MALVOLIO: "Besides, you waste your precious time with a foolish knight."

SIR ANDREW: He's talking about me, I tell you!

MALVOLIO: "One Sir Andrew."

SIR ANDREW: I *knew* it was me. Many people call me a fool.

MALVOLIO *(picking up the letter)*: What's this?

FABIAN: Now the bird is near the trap.

SIR TOBY: May he be inspired to read it aloud!

MALVOLIO: By my life, this is my lady's handwriting. *(Reading)* *To the unknown beloved: this letter and my good wishes.* Her very phrases. *(He breaks the wax seal.)* It has her personal seal on it. Yes, it's from my lady, all right. To whom has it been sent?

FABIAN: This will convince him, heart and soul.

MALVOLIO *(reading)*: *God knows I love,*
But who?
Lips, do not move,
No man must know.

What if it should be you, Malvolio?

SIR TOBY: Be hanged, you braggart!

MALVOLIO: *Silence cuts me like a knife,*
M, O, A, I, does rule my life.

SIR TOBY: Excellent woman, I say.

FABIAN: What poison she has served him!

SIR TOBY: And how quickly he takes the bait!

MALVOLIO: Now she writes in prose.
I may command where I adore.
Why, she may command me! I serve her—
she is my lady. What do those letters mean?
M, O, A, I—all those letters are in my
name, but not in that order.

43

If this letter falls into your hand, consider. By the chance of fortune, I am above you, but do not be afraid of greatness! Some are born great, some achieve greatness, and some have greatness thrust upon them. The fates offer their helping hands. Let your courage and spirit embrace them. To prepare yourself for what you are likely to be, cast off your humble exterior and appear fresh. Be openly hostile to a certain kinsman and rude with servants. Let your speech be about lofty matters. Be original. She who sighs for you gives you this advice. Remember who complimented you on your yellow stockings. I say, remember. Go on, your fortune is made, if you want it to be. If not, you can stay a steward forever, the friend of servants, and not worthy to touch Fortune's fingers. Farewell. She who would be your servant. —The Fortunate-Unhappy

This is as plain as daylight! I will be proud. I will read important authors, I will clash with Sir Toby. I will avoid my common friends. Everything points to this: My lady loves me. She did praise my yellow stockings recently. In this way *(he waves the letter)*, she tells me of her love and encourages me to act in ways she likes. I thank my lucky stars that I am so lucky in

love. I will be aloof and proud, in yellow
stockings as fast as I can put them on.
(He turns the letter over.) Here is a postscript:
*You cannot help but know who I am. If you
love me, too, show it by smiling. You have
such a lovely smile. So in my presence, smile,
my dear sweetheart, I beg you.*
I will smile. I will do all she asks.

(Malvolio exits.)

FABIAN: I wouldn't give up my part in this sport
for a pension paid by the shah of Persia!

SIR TOBY: I could marry the girl for this hoax.

SIR ANDREW: So could I!

SIR TOBY: And ask no other dowry from her
but another such joke.

(Maria enters.)

FABIAN: Here comes our noble jokester!

SIR TOBY: When he comes out of his dream,
He'll go mad, for sure!

MARIA: Tell the truth. Do you think it
worked?

SIR TOBY: Without question!

MARIA: If you want to see the joke play out,
watch him when he first sees my lady.
He will come to her in yellow stockings,
a color she hates. He will smile at her,

which will be so opposite to her mood.
You know how inclined she is to sadness.
How annoyed she will be! If you want to
see it, follow me!

SIR TOBY: Lead on, you excellent jokester!

SIR ANDREW: I'll go, too.

*(**All** exit.)*

ACT 3

| Scene 1 |

Olivia's garden. **Viola** *enters, and* **Feste** *with a small drum.*

VIOLA: Greetings, friend, and your music. Do you live by your drumming?

FESTE: No, sir, I live by the church.

VIOLA: Are you a preacher?

FESTE: No, sir. I live by the church, for I live in my house, and my house is near the church.

VIOLA: So you could just as well say the king lives by begging, if a beggar lives near him. Or the church is near your drum if the drum happens to be near the church.

FESTE: You said it, sir! Such are the times! A sentence is just a kid glove to a man with a quick wit. It can so easily be turned inside out!

VIOLA: I can see you're a merry fellow and care about nothing.

FESTE: Not so, sir. I do care for something. But upon my conscience, sir, I do not care for you. If that's caring about nothing, sir, I wish it would make you invisible.

VIOLA: Aren't you the Lady Olivia's fool?

FESTE: No, indeed, sir. Lady Olivia does not enjoy entertainment. She will not keep a fool, sir, until she is married. A fool is to a husband as a sardine is to a herring— the husband's the bigger. I am, indeed, not her fool, but her corrupter of words.

VIOLA: I saw you recently at Count Orsino's.

FESTE: I think I saw your wise self there, too.

VIOLA: If you make fun of me, I'll stay with you no longer. Wait. *(She looks in her purse.)* Here's something for you. *(She gives him some money.)*
Is your lady inside?

FESTE: The lady is inside, sir. I will let her know you are here.

(Feste exits.)

VIOLA: He's wise enough to be a paid fool.
And, to do that well, requires intelligence.
He must observe the moods of those
He jokes about. This is a job requiring as much hard work
As the profession of a wise man.
When it's done intelligently, his fooling
Is fit and proper. But when a wise man
Stoops to folly, he ruins his reputation.

(Sir Toby Belch and Sir Andrew Aguecheek enter.)

SIR TOBY: God be with you, gentleman.

VIOLA: And you, sir.

SIR TOBY: Will you come into the house? My niece wishes for you to enter, if your trade is with her.

VIOLA: I do wish to see your niece, sir.

(Olivia and Maria come out of the house to meet her. Viola begins one of her prepared speeches.)

Most excellent accomplished lady,
May the heavens rain favors on you!
I've a message meant for your ears alone.

OLIVIA *(to the others)***:** Let the garden door be shut, and then leave us alone.

(Sir Toby, Sir Andrew, and Maria exit.)

Give me your hand, sir. *(She offers hers.)*

VIOLA: *(taking it and bowing)***:** Fair princess,
I am your humble servant, Cesario.

OLIVIA: My servant, sir!
You are servant to the Count Orsino.

VIOLA: As he is yours. And what is his
Must also belong to you. Your servant's
Servant is your servant, madam.

OLIVIA: As for him, I don't think about him.
As for his thoughts, I wish they were blanks
Rather than filled with me!

VIOLA: Madam, I am here to make you think
More kindly of him.

OLIVIA: Oh, please, I beg you,

Don't ever speak of him again.
But if you insist on pleading,
I'd rather hear it
Than music from the heavens.
After your last enchanting visit,
I sent a ring after you. In doing that,
I wronged myself, my servant, and,
I fear—you. I must accept your bad opinion
Of me for forcing that ring on you in
Such a shameful way. What must you think?

VIOLA: I pity you.

OLIVIA: That's a step toward love.

VIOLA: No, not even a small step. It's well-known
That very often we pity enemies.

OLIVIA: Well, then, I think it's time I learn
To smile again.

(A clock strikes.)

The clock reminds me of the waste of time.
Fear not, good youth. I will not pursue you.
And yet, when you come to maturity,
Your wife will have a good man.
(She points toward the setting sun.) There is
your route: due west.

VIOLA: Then westward ho!
Blessings and a good life to your ladyship.
You have no message for my lord?

OLIVIA: Stay a moment. May I ask you
What you think of me?

VIOLA: *(speaking in a riddle)*: That you think you are what you are not. *(She means, "You think you love a man, but you do not.")*

OLIVIA *(assuming Viola is being rude)*: If I think so, I think the same of you. *(She means, "I think you are rude.")*

VIOLA: Then you think right. I am not what I appear to be. *(She means, "I'm a woman.")*

OLIVIA: I wish you were as I want you to be! *(She means, "I wish you were my husband!")*

VIOLA: Would it be better than I am now? I hope so, for you are making me look silly.

OLIVIA: *(to herself)*: Oh, how handsome he looks When he is angry! Love that tries to hide itself Is exposed sooner than the crime of murder. Love is as plain as daylight. *(aloud)* Cesario, by the roses of the spring, Maidenhood, honor, truth, and everything, I love you so much that I cannot hide it. Don't draw any wrong conclusions from my Words of love. You have given me No reason to woo you. Think of it this way: Love that's sought after is good, but Love that is given unsought is better.

VIOLA: I swear that my heart, my loyalty, And my truth belong to me. No woman has, Or ever will have, a share in it, except me. And so goodbye, good madam. I'll never again

Plead with you for my tearful master.

OLIVIA: Do come again. Maybe you'll be able
To move my heart to welcome his love.

(**Olivia** and **Viola** exit.)

| Scene 2 |

A room in Olivia's house. **Sir Toby Belch, Sir Andrew Aguecheek,** *and* **Fabian** *enter.*

SIR ANDREW: No, I won't stay any longer.

SIR TOBY: But why, Sir Andrew?

SIR ANDREW: Well, I saw your niece being nicer to the count's servant than she has ever been to me. I saw it in the garden.

SIR TOBY: Did she see you there, old boy?

SIR ANDREW: As plain as I see you now.

FABIAN: Then it is clear that she did it just to make you jealous. You should have picked a fight with the youth. Now you look weak in her eyes. You'll have to do something soon.

SIR TOBY: Challenge the count's servant to a duel. Hurt him in eleven places. My niece will get to hear of it. A report of your courage will raise her opinion of you.

FABIAN: There is no other way, Sir Andrew.

SIR ANDREW: Will either of you deliver the

challenge to him?

SIR TOBY: Go, write it in a strong handwriting. Be sharp and to the point. Off you go!

SIR ANDREW: Where shall I find you?

SIR TOBY: We'll meet you at the writing room. Go.

(Sir Andrew exits.)

FABIAN: He's your dear little puppet, Sir Toby.

SIR TOBY: I have been dear to him, lad—I've cost him some two thousand pounds or so.

FABIAN: We shall have quite a letter from him. Will you deliver it?

SIR TOBY: If I don't, never trust me again. And I'll do my best to get the youth to respond, though I think even oxen and ropes couldn't pull them together.

FABIAN: And his opponent, the youth, has no mark of cruelty in his face.

(Maria enters.)

SIR TOBY: Look, here comes our young bird.

MARIA: If you want a big laugh, follow me. That idiot Malvolio is wearing yellow stockings! He obeys every point in the letter that I wrote. He smiles until his face cracks. You've never seen such a sight! I can hardly resist hurling things at him. I know my lady will strike him. If she does, he'll smile and take it as a great favor.

SIR TOBY: Come on, take us to him!

(***All** exit.*)

| Scene 3 |

*A street. **Antonio** and **Sebastian** enter.*

SEBASTIAN: I didn't mean to trouble you,
But since you enjoy putting yourself out,
I won't scold you anymore.

ANTONIO: I couldn't stay behind. I worried
About your safety. These lands
Often prove dangerous to a stranger
Without a guide or a friend.

SEBASTIAN: My kind Antonio!
I can make no other answer but thanks.
If I were as rich as I am indebted to you,
You would be richly rewarded.
What shall we do?
Shall we go see the sights of this town?

ANTONIO: Tomorrow, sir. It's best to find your
lodgings first.

SEBASTIAN: I am not tired, and it's still very early.
Let's do some sightseeing.

ANTONIO: If I may be excused—I walk

These streets in some danger.
Once, in a sea fight against the count's ships,
I played a big part. So big, in fact,
That if I were found here, I'd have no chance.

SEBASTIAN: You killed many of his people?

ANTONIO: The offense was not so bloody.
It could be settled by repaying what we took
From them. In fact, in the interest of trade,
Most of our city's people did.
I'm the only one who didn't.
For that—if I'm found here—I shall
  pay dearly.

SEBASTIAN: Don't walk about too openly, then.

ANTONIO: Here's my purse. It's best to lodge
In the south suburbs, at the Elephant Inn.
I'll order our meal while you go sightseeing.
You'll find me there.

SEBASTIAN: Why should I take your purse?

ANTONIO: Perhaps you'll see some souvenir
You'd like to buy. I don't imagine you have
Much extra money for luxuries, sir.

SEBASTIAN: I'll carry your purse and leave you
  for an hour.

ANTONIO: To the Elephant . . .

SEBASTIAN: I'll remember.

*(**All** exit.)*

| Scene 4 |

*Olivia's garden. **Olivia** and **Maria** enter.*

OLIVIA (*to herself*)**:** I have sent for him.
   He says he'll come. How shall I entertain him?
   What should I give him? For youth is
      more often bought than begged or
      borrowed.
   I'm speaking too loudly.
   (*to Maria*) Where's Malvolio?
   He is serious and formal—good qualities
   In a servant, considering my situation.
   Where is Malvolio?

MARIA: He's coming, madam:
   But very strangely. He seems possessed.

OLIVIA: Why, what's the matter? Is he raving?

MARIA: No, madam, he does nothing but smile.
   Your ladyship had best have her guard up.
   I'm sure the man has lost his wits.

OLIVIA: Go and get him.

*(**Maria** leaves.)*

   I'm as mad as he is—if sad madness
   And merry madness are equal.

*(**Malvolio** enters.)*

   Greetings, Malvolio.

MALVOLIO (*smiling broadly*)**:** Sweet lady, hello.

56

OLIVIA: Are you smiling? I sent for you because I am sad.

MALVOLIO: Sad, lady? Why so sad? Haven't you noticed my yellow stockings? Surely, they should please your eye.

OLIVIA: What's the matter with you?

MALVOLIO: Not full of black thoughts, though my legs are yellow. The commands of the letter will be carried out. We know the sweet Roman handwriting.

OLIVIA: You're acting strangely, Malvolio.

MARIA: How are you, Malvolio?

MALVOLIO: Are you talking to me? Do nightingales answer crows?

MARIA: Why do you appear before my lady with such ridiculous boldness?

MALVOLIO (to Olivia): *Do not be afraid of greatness*—oh, that was well-written.

OLIVIA: What are you talking about, Malvolio?

MALVOLIO: *Some are born great—*

OLIVIA: What?

MALVOLIO: *Some achieve greatness—*

OLIVIA: What are you saying?

MALVOLIO: *And some have greatness thrust upon them—*

OLIVIA: May heaven cure you!

This is truly midsummer madness!

*(A **servant** enters.)*

SERVANT: Madam, Count Orsino's young gentleman has returned. It was hard to persuade him to come back. He awaits your lady's pleasure.

OLIVIA: I'll come to him.

*(**Servant** exits.)*

Good Maria, let this fellow be tended. *(She gestures toward Malvolio.)* Where is my cousin Toby? Some of my people must take special care of him. He must not come to harm for half of my fortune.

*(**Olivia** and **Maria** exit.)*

MALVOLIO: Oh, ho! It's becoming clearer and clearer. No less a man than Sir Toby to look after me! This goes right along with the letter. As she wrote, she is sending him on purpose, so I can be "openly hostile" to him. It all makes sense. Not one grain of doubt, no obstacle, nothing to come between me and the fulfillment of my hopes! Well, Jove, not I, has done this, and he is to be thanked!

*(**Maria** returns with **Sir Toby Belch** and **Fabian**.)*

SIR TOBY: Where is he, in the name of all that's holy?

FABIAN: Here he is, here he is. *(to Malvolio)* How are you, sir?

MALVOLIO: Go away. I reject you. Let me enjoy my privacy. Be gone!

MARIA: Look how strangely he's acting! It's as if he's possessed by the devil. Didn't I tell you? Sir Toby, my lady wants you to treat him with care.

MALVOLIO: Ah, ha! Does she really?

SIR TOBY *(to Maria and Fabian)***:** Stop! We must deal gently with him. Leave it to me. *(to Malvolio)* How do you do, Malvolio? How is everything? Defy the devil! Remember, he's the enemy of mankind.

MALVOLIO: Do you know what you are saying?

MARIA *(to Sir Toby and Fabian)***:** Just notice, if you speak ill of the devil, how personally he takes it. Pray God he isn't bewitched.

SIR TOBY: Please, do be quiet. Don't you see how you are annoying him? Leave him to me.

FABIAN: You must use gentleness. Gently! Gently! The devil is violent, and he won't be treated roughly!

SIR TOBY *(to Malvolio)***:** Why, hello there, my little bird. How are you, chick?

MALVOLIO: Sir?

SIR TOBY: Yes, duckie, come with me. What, man!

It's not wise for a smart fellow like you
to play games with Satan. Hang him, that
foul creature from the underworld!

MARIA: Get him to say his prayers, good Sir
Toby. Get him to pray.

MALVOLIO: My prayers?

MARIA: No, I tell you—he will not hear of
godliness.

MALVOLIO: Go and hang yourselves, all of you
idle good-for-nothings! I am not like you.
You shall know more of me later.

(Malvolio exits.)

SIR TOBY: Is it possible?

FABIAN: If this were a stage play, I'd call it
unlikely fiction!

SIR TOBY: He has fallen for the joke—hook,
line, and sinker, man!

MARIA: But follow him at once, in case the
joke goes sour.

SIR TOBY: Here's an idea: We'll put him in a
dark room in a straitjacket. My niece
already believes that he's mad. We may
carry the joke that far, for our pleasure
and his pain, until we decide to have
mercy on him. But see who's here!

*(**Sir Andrew Aguecheek** enters, waving a piece of paper.)*

FABIAN: More fun to come!

SIR ANDREW: Here's the challenge. Read it. I promise you there's vinegar and pepper in it.

SIR TOBY: Give it to me. *(He reads.) Youth, whoever you are, you are a scurvy fellow. Don't wonder why I call you that, for I will give you no reason for it.*

FABIAN: A good touch. That keeps you within the law.

SIR TOBY: *You come to the Lady Olivia, and in front of me she treats you kindly. But you lie in your teeth. That's not the reason I'm challenging you. I will waylay you on your way home. If you have the good luck to kill me, you'd be killing me like a rogue and a villain.*

FABIAN: You're still keeping on the right side of the law. Good.

SIR TOBY: *Farewell, and may God have mercy on one of our souls! He may have mercy on mine, so look to yourself. Your friend, as you treat him, and your sworn enemy, Andrew Aguecheek.* If this letter does not move him, his legs cannot. I'll give it to him.

MARIA: Good timing! He is now talking with my lady, and will leave soon.

SIR TOBY: Go, Sir Andrew. Wait for him at the

corner of the garden. As soon as you see him, draw your sword and swear horribly. A terrible oath spoken with swaggering self-confidence does more for a man's reputation than an actual swordfight. Go on, now!

SIR ANDREW: You can leave the swearing to me!

*(**Sir Andrew** exits.)*

SIR TOBY *(to Fabian)***:** I won't deliver Sir Andrew's letter to the young gentleman. He'll know it was written by a blockhead, and it won't scare him. Instead, I will deliver the challenge by word of mouth. I'll make Aguecheek out to be very brave. The young gentleman will fear his rage, skill, and fury. Both will be so frightened that they will kill each other by exchanging looks!

*(**Olivia** and **Viola** enter.)*

FABIAN: Here he comes with your niece. Stand aside till he leaves. Then follow him.

SIR TOBY: Meanwhile, I'll think about some horrid message for the challenge.

*(**Sir Toby**, **Fabian**, and **Maria** exit.)*

OLIVIA: I have said too much to a heart of stone,
And laid my honor too carelessly on it.
I fear I did wrong, but I was pushed to it
By strong passion.

VIOLA: My master's grief is just as strong as
your passion.

OLIVIA *(to Viola)***:** Here, wear this locket for me.
It has my picture inside.
Don't refuse it. It has no tongue to annoy you.
And, I beg you, come again tomorrow.
What could you ask of me that I would deny,
As long as it's honorable?

VIOLA: Nothing but this, your true love for
my master.

OLIVIA: How could I honorably give him that
When I have already given it to you?

VIOLA: I will release you.

OLIVIA: Well, come again tomorrow.
Farewell for now.

*(Olivia exits. **Sir Toby Belch** and **Fabian** return.)*

SIR TOBY: Gentleman, God save you.

VIOLA: And you, sir.

SIR TOBY: Whatever weapons you have, get them ready. I don't know what wrongs you did to him, but your challenger is as bloodthirsty as a hunting dog. He's waiting for you by the garden. Draw your sword and get ready quickly, for your opponent is fast, skillful, and deadly.

VIOLA: You must be mistaken, sir. I am sure no man has any quarrel with me. My memory is free and clear of offense done to anyone.

SIR TOBY: You'll find it otherwise, I assure you. If you value your life, take up your guard. Your opponent has all the gifts of youth, strength, skill, and anger.

VIOLA: I ask you, sir, who is he?

SIR TOBY: He is a knight, dubbed with a ceremonial sword as he knelt on a carpet. But he is a devil in a private brawl. He's killed three people, and now is so angry that only a death and burial will satisfy him. "Strike first" is his motto, take it or leave it.

VIOLA: I'll go back to the house and ask the

lady for protection. I am no fighter.
I've heard of some men who pick fights
on purpose just to test their valor.
He must be such a man.

SIR TOBY: Sir, *no*! His anger stems from a very
real cause. So you'd better get on with it
and give him his satisfaction. You shall
not go back to the house unless you cross
swords with me. Therefore, go on—or
raise your sword against me. You must
fight—that's for certain—or stop
carrying a weapon.

VIOLA: This is as rude as it is strange! I beg
you, tell me how I offended this knight.
Surely it's something to do with an
oversight, nothing done on purpose.

SIR TOBY: I'll do so. Mister Fabian, stay with
this gentleman until I return.

*(**Sir Toby** exits.)*

VIOLA: Please, sir, do you know of this matter?

FABIAN: I know the knight is incensed against
you. He wants it settled in a fight to the
death. I don't know any other details.

VIOLA: I beg you, what kind of man is he?

FABIAN: To look at him, you wouldn't see
the great promise he shows in action.
He is indeed, sir, the most skillful,

bloody, and fatal opponent in Illyria.
Will you meet him halfway? I'll make
your peace with him if I can.

VIOLA: I shall be indebted to you for it.

*(They go. Viola is very frightened. **Sir Toby** and **Sir
Andrew** return.)*

SIR TOBY: Why, man, he's a very devil!
I've never seen such a fighter! He strikes as
firmly as your feet hit the ground they step
on. They say he's been a fencer for the shah
of Persia.

SIR ANDREW: A pox on it, I won't duel with him!

SIR TOBY: Yes, but he won't be calmed down.
Fabian can hardly hold him back.

SIR ANDREW: Blast it! If I'd thought he was so
brave and cunning in fencing, I'd never
have challenged him. If he'll let the matter
slide, I'll give him my horse, Gray Capilet.

SIR TOBY: I'll see what he says. Stay here, do your
best, and this will end without someone's
death. *(to himself)* Yes, indeed, I'll take your
horse for a ride as well as you!

*(**Fabian** and **Viola** enter again.)*

SIR TOBY *(to Fabian)*: I have his horse to settle
the quarrel. I have persuaded him the
youth's a devil.

FABIAN *(to Sir Toby)*: He's as pale as if a bear were chasing him!

SIR TOBY *(to Viola)*: There's no remedy, sir. He'll fight you because he's sworn to. But he's had second thoughts about the quarrel. Now he thinks it was hardly worth talking about. But he means to go ahead with the fight to support his vow. He promises he will not hurt you.

VIOLA *(aside)*: Pray God defend me! I'm tempted to tell them that I'm not a man!

FABIAN: Retreat if you see him furious.

SIR TOBY *(to Sir Andrew)*: Come on, Sir Andrew, there's no remedy. The gentleman will have one bout with you for the sake of his honor. By the rules of dueling, he can't avoid it. But he has promised not to hurt you. Come on. Get going!

SIR ANDREW: Pray God he keeps his promise! *(He draws his sword nervously.)*

VIOLA: I do assure you this is against my will. *(She draws her sword nervously. They both close their eyes and wave their swords around. Antonio enters and sees them apparently fighting. He thinks Viola is Sebastian.)*

ANTONIO *(to Sir Andrew)*: Put up your sword! If this young gentleman has offended you, I'll answer for him. If you have offended him,

On his behalf, I defy you. *(Antonio draws his sword expertly.)*

SIR TOBY: You, sir! Who are you?

ANTONIO: One who stands up for his friend!

SIR TOBY: Well, if you're a stand-in, I'm ready for you! *(Sir Toby draws.)*

FABIAN: Stop, Sir Toby! Stop! Here come the officers of the law!

*(**Two officers** enter.)*

SIR TOBY *(to Antonio)*: We'll continue this later.

VIOLA *(to Sir Andrew)*: Please, sir, put up your sword, I beg you.

SIR ANDREW *(relieved)*: Indeed I will, sir, and I'll keep my promise. Capilet will carry you easily. He responds well to the rein.

FIRST OFFICER *(pointing to Antonio)*: This is the man. Do your duty.

SECOND OFFICER: Antonio, I arrest you on order of Count Orsino.

ANTONIO: You're making a mistake, sir!

FIRST OFFICER: No, sir, no mistake. I know you, Though you have no sailor's cap on your head. Take him away. He knows I know him well.

ANTONIO: I'll go quietly. *(to Viola)* This comes From seeking you. But there's no remedy. I'll have to answer for it. What will you do,

Now that I must ask for my purse back?
The fact that I cannot help you grieves me
Even more than my own fate.
You look astonished, but be of good cheer.

SECOND OFFICER: Come away, sir.

ANTONIO: I must ask you for that money.

VIOLA: What money, sir?
For the kindness you have just showed me,
And partly because of your present trouble,
I'll lend you some money. I don't have much.
Here, take half of what I have.

ANTONIO (*angrily*): Will you refuse me now?
Is it possible that what I've done for you
Counts for nothing?

VIOLA: I don't know what you're talking about.
I've never seen you before in my life.

ANTONIO: Oh, sweet heaven!

SECOND OFFICER: Come, sir, it's time to go.

ANTONIO: Let me speak a little. This youth—
I snatched him from the jaws of death,
I helped him with a holy love, and was
devoted to his very image.

FIRST OFFICER: What's that to us? We're wasting
time. Let's go.

ANTONIO: But, oh, how wretched an idol he is!
Sebastian, you have brought
Shame on your good looks. In nature,

There's no fault worse than that of the mind.
Only the unkind can be called deformed.
Virtue is beauty, but those who are
Beautiful to look at, although evil inside,
Are empty boxes overfilled by the devil.

FIRST OFFICER: The man's mad! Come on, sir.

ANTONIO: Lead me on.

(Officers and Antonio exit.)

VIOLA *(realizing what Antonio has been saying)*:
Dear brother, could it be true
That I have now been taken for you?
He called me "Sebastian." My mirror tells me
We look exactly alike. I have
Copied his style for my disguise.
Oh, if it's true that he is still alive,
Tempests are kind, and full of love!

(Viola exits.)

SIR TOBY: A very dishonorable boy!
He refused to help his friend in need.
And as for his cowardice, ask Fabian.

FABIAN: Yes, a coward, a total coward.

SIR ANDREW: By God, I'll chase after him again
and beat him!

SIR TOBY: Do—beat him up soundly, but don't
draw your sword.

SIR ANDREW: If I don't—

(Sir Andrew exits.)

FABIAN: Come on, let's see what happens.

SIR TOBY: I'll bet that nothing will happen.

(All exit.)

ACT 4

| Scene 1 |

*The street before Olivia's house. **Sebastian** and **Feste** enter.*

FESTE: Are you trying to pretend that I wasn't looking for you?

SEBASTIAN: Go away. You are a foolish fellow. Let me be rid of you!

FESTE: You're keeping this up very well. *(sarcastically)* No, I do not know you. I wasn't sent to you by my lady, who wants to speak with you. And your name is not Cesario. And this isn't even my own nose! Nothing that is so is so!

SEBASTIAN: Please, spout your nonsense somewhere else. You don't know me.

FESTE: Spout my nonsense! What are you talking about? I beg you now, don't be so strange. Tell me what I should say to my lady. Shall I tell her that you are coming?

SEBASTIAN: I beg you, you fool, leave me. Here's some money for you. If you stay longer, I'll give you something worse!

FESTE: Upon my word, you are very generous. Wise men who give money to fools

Get themselves very well-regarded—
Even 14 years later.

(Sir Andrew, Sir Toby, and Fabian enter.)

SIR ANDREW *(thinking that Sebastian is Viola)*: Now,
sir, so we meet again! This is for you!
(He strikes Sebastian.)

SEBASTIAN *(striking back)*: And this is for you!
And this! And this! Is everyone here mad?

SIR TOBY: Stop that, sir, or I'll throw your
dagger over the house.

FESTE: I will tell my lady about this right away.
I wouldn't be in your shoes for two cents!

(Feste exits.)

SIR TOBY *(holding Sebastian)*: Come on, sir. Stop!

SIR ANDREW: No, let him alone. I'll get at him
another way. I'll take him to court on a
battery charge, if there is any law in
Illyria. Though I struck him first, that
doesn't matter.

SEBASTIAN *(to Sir Toby)*: Take your hands off me!

SIR TOBY: Come, sir, I will not let you go.

(Sebastian struggles free.)

SEBASTIAN: Now, what do you have to say?
If you dare to go further, draw your
sword! *(Sebastian draws his own sword.)*

SIR TOBY: What, what? Well then, I must have
an ounce or two of your rude blood.

*(Sir Toby draws his sword. **Olivia** enters.)*

OLIVIA: Stop, Toby!

SIR TOBY: Madam?

OLIVIA: Must it always be like this? You wretch,
Fit for the mountains and barbarous caves,
Where manners were never taught!
Out of my sight!
(to Sebastian, thinking he is Viola) Dear Cesario,
Do not be offended.
(to Sir Toby) You brute! Get out of here!

*(**Sir Toby, Sir Andrew,** and **Fabian** exit.)*

(to Sebastian) Gentle friend, let wisdom, not
Anger, guide your reaction to this
Rude attack on your peace. Come
To my house and I'll tell you how many
Pointless pranks this brute has had a hand in.
Then you'll be able to smile at this one.
Shame on his soul!
He gave my half of your heart a shock.

SEBASTIAN *(totally puzzled, not knowing Olivia)*:
What is going on? What's the idea?
Am I mad, or is this a dream?
(He sees that Olivia has strong feelings for him.)
If this is a dream, let me stay asleep.

OLIVIA: Please come with me. I wish you would.

SEBASTIAN: Madam, I will.

OLIVIA: Oh, wonderful!

*(**All** exit.)*

| Scene 2 |

A room in Olivia's house. **Maria** *and* **Feste** *enter.*

MARIA: Now then, put on this gown and this beard. Make him believe you are Sir Topas, the parson. Do it quickly while I call Sir Toby.

*(**Maria** exits.)*

FESTE: Well, I'll put it on to disguise myself. I wish I were the first man who'd ever practiced deceit in such a gown!

*(**Sir Toby Belch** and **Maria** enter.)*

SIR TOBY: God bless you, Master Parson.

FESTE: Good day to you, Sir Toby.

SIR TOBY *(pointing to a door with a small grille to allow conversation)*: Tend to him, Sir Topas.

FESTE *(in a fake voice)*: Hello there, I say! God's peace in this prison!

MALVOLIO *(from an inner room, weakly)*: Who's calling?

FESTE: Sir Topas, the parson, who comes to visit Malvolio, the lunatic.

75

MALVOLIO: Sir Topas, Sir Topas, good Sir Topas—go to my lady.

FESTE: Don't you talk about anything but ladies?

SIR TOBY: Well said, Master Parson.

MALVOLIO: Sir Topas, never was a man so wronged. Please, do not think that I am mad, yet They keep me here in hideous darkness.

FESTE: Are you saying that place is dark?

MALVOLIO: It is pitch black, Sir Topas!

FESTE: Why, it has bay windows as clear as shutters, and the high windows toward the south-north are as bright as ebony. Yet you complain of darkness?

MALVOLIO: I am not mad, Sir Topas. I tell you this place is dark.

FESTE: Madman, you are in error. I say there is no darkness but ignorance, and you are stuck in it.

MALVOLIO: I say this house is as dark as ignorance, and I say there was never a man so abused. I am no more mad than you are! Test me by asking some searching questions.

FESTE: What did Pythagoras think of wild birds?

MALVOLIO: That the soul of one's grandmother might possibly inhabit a bird.

FESTE: What do you think of that?

MALVOLIO: I think that the soul is noble.
I do not agree with Pythagoras.

FESTE: Farewell. Remain in darkness. You
must agree with Pythagoras before I will
declare you sane. You must be afraid of
killing a bird for fear of displacing your
grandmother's soul. Farewell.

MALVOLIO: Sir Topas! Sir Topas!

SIR TOBY: My dear Sir Topas!

FESTE *(to Sir Toby)***:** I'm a good actor!

MARIA: You could have done this without the
disguise. He can't see you.

SIR TOBY: Talk to him in your own voice, and
then come and tell me how you find him.
(to Maria) I wish we were rid of this practical
joking. If he can easily be set free, I wish
he were. I'm far out of favor with my niece!
No, I cannot keep playing this joke.
Come to my room by and by.

*(**Sir Toby** and **Maria** exit.)*

FESTE *(singing in his own voice outside Malvolio's
door)***:** Hey, Robin, jolly Robin,
Tell me how your lady is.

MALVOLIO: Fool—

FESTE: My lady loves another—Who's calling?

MALVOLIO: Good fool, do me a favor.
Get me a candle, a pen, ink, and paper.

As I am a gentleman, I'll live to show my thanks to you.

FESTE: Master Malvolio!

MALVOLIO: Yes, good fool.

FESTE: Alas, sir. How did you come to be insane?

MALVOLIO: Fool, there was never a man so terribly abused. I am as sane as you are.

FESTE: As sane as I am? Then you are indeed mad, if you are no saner than a fool.

MALVOLIO: They have put me here, kept me in darkness, and sent parsons to me. They do all they can to drive me out of my wits.

FESTE: Take care what you say. The parson is here. *(in his Sir Topas voice)* Malvolio, may the heavens restore your wits! Try to sleep, and stop jabbering nonsense.

MALVOLIO: Sir Topas—

FESTE *(still as Sir Topas)***:** Don't talk to him, good fellow. *(his own voice)* Who, I, sir? Not I, sir. God be with you, good Sir Topas. *(Sir Topas again)* Yes, indeed. Amen. *(his own voice)* I will, sir, I will.

MALVOLIO: Fool, fool, fool, I say—

FESTE: Sir, be patient. What do you want? I'm in trouble for speaking to you.

MALVOLIO: Good fool, help me get some light and some paper. I promise you that I'm as sane as any man in Illyria.

FESTE: I wish that you were, sir!

MALVOLIO: By this hand, I am. Give me some ink, paper, and light, and take what I will write to my lady. It shall profit you more than the delivery of any other letter.

FESTE: I will help you. But tell me the truth. Are you really mad, or are you pretending?

MALVOLIO: Believe me, I am not. I tell the truth.

FESTE: No. I'll never believe a madman till I see his brains. I'll get you light and paper and ink.

MALVOLIO: I'll reward you well. Please go now.

FESTE *(singing)*: I am gone, sir. But soon, sir, I will be back again.

*(**Feste** exits.)*

| Scene 3 |

*Olivia's garden. **Sebastian** enters. He still can't believe he's not dreaming.*

SEBASTIAN: This is the air. That's the glorious sun.
This pearl she gave me, I can feel it and see it.
And though I'm filled with wonder, this is
Surely not madness. So where's Antonio?
I could not find him at the Elephant,
Yet he had been there. They told me that

He looked for me all over town.
Now his advice might be worth gold!
This accidental flood of good fortune is
So strange. I argue with my own mind
When it tries to tell me I am not mad.
Or else the lady's mad. But if that were so,
She couldn't rule her house and her servants,
    or manage her affairs
So smoothly and with such confidence.
I don't understand it. But here comes the lady!

(Olivia and a priest enter.)

OLIVIA: Don't blame me for this haste.
    If you mean well, go with me and the priest
    Into the nearby chapel. Before him
    And under that holy roof, pledge me
    Your vows of love in marriage. Then
    My jealous and doubtful soul may live at peace.
    He shall keep it a secret until you are willing
    To make it public. Then we'll have
    A celebration in keeping with my rank.
    What do you say?

SEBASTIAN: I'll follow this man, and go with you;
    And, having made vows, will ever be true.

OLIVIA: Then lead the way, good father.
    And may the heavens shine
    In blessing of this act of mine!

(Olivia, Sebastian, and priest exit.)

ACT 5

| Scene 1 |

The street before Olivia's house. **Feste** *and* **Fabian** *enter.*

FABIAN: Please let me see his letter.

FESTE: Please do not ask to see it.

FABIAN: That's like giving someone a dog and then asking for it back again.

*(**Duke**, **Viola**, and **attendants** enter.)*

DUKE: Are you Lady Olivia's men, friends?
  Please let your lady know I am here.

FESTE: Gladly, sir.

*(**Feste** exits. **Antonio** and **officers** enter.)*

VIOLA: Here comes the man who rescued me.

DUKE: I remember that face well,
  Even though when I saw it last
  It was smeared black in the
  Smoke of war. He was captain of
    a small vessel
  That wasn't worth much. He fought so well
  Against the finest ship in our fleet
  That even those who suffered great losses
  Proclaimed his fame and honor.
  (to the officers) What has he done?

81

FIRST OFFICER: Orsino, this is the Antonio who
    Took the *Phoenix* and her cargo from Crete.
    He's the one who boarded the *Tiger* when
    Your young nephew Titus lost his leg.
    We arrested him here in the streets where
    He was involved in a private brawl.

VIOLA: He did me a kindness, sir, by drawing
    His sword to defend me. After that,
    He said some nonsensical things
    So I assumed he was mad.

DUKE: Famous pirate! Thief of the high seas!
    What foolish boldness brought you here,
    At the mercy of your enemies?

ANTONIO: Orsino, noble sir, allow me
    To shake off those names you call me.
    Antonio was never a thief or pirate—though
    There are reasons to be your enemy.
    Witchcraft drew me here.
    I rescued that most ungrateful boy,
    He who is there by your side.
    I plucked him from the angry sea.
    He was a wreck past hope. I gave him his life
    And added to it my love. For his sake,
    I exposed myself to danger in this town.
    I drew my sword to defend him from attack.
    When I was arrested, his false cunning led him
    To deny our friendship to my face.
    In the time it takes to blink, he'd turned into

Someone who'd not seen me for 20 years.
He denied me my own purse, which
I'd given him not half an hour before.

VIOLA *(astonished)*: How can this be?

DUKE *(to the officers)*: When did he arrive here?

ANTONIO *(answering for himself)*: Today, my lord.
For three months before this, we'd been
Together day and night, without a break
Of so much as a minute.

*(**Olivia** and **attendants** enter.)*

DUKE: Here comes the countess.
Now heaven walks on earth!
(to Antonio) As for you, you speak madness.
For the past three months this youth
Has been my servant. But more of that later.
(to the officers) Take him to one side.

OLIVIA: What does my lord wish—other than
What he cannot have—that Olivia can
supply?
*(She sees Viola, mistaking her for her new
husband.)* Cesario, you are not keeping
your promise.

VIOLA *(not understanding)*: Madam?

DUKE: Gracious Olivia—

OLIVIA: What do you say, Cesario? *(seeing the
duke start to speak, she stops him)*
Please, my lord—

VIOLA: My lord wishes to speak.
   Duty demands that I remain silent.

OLIVIA: If it's your same old tune, my lord,
   It sounds to me like howling.

DUKE: Still so cruel?

OLIVIA: Still so consistent, my lord.

DUKE: Consistently *perverse*! You rude lady,
   At whose ungrateful altars my soul
   Has offered the most faithful prayers!
   What shall I do?

OLIVIA: Whatever pleases you, my lord.

DUKE: Listen to this. Since you refuse my love,
   And because I think I know
   What has replaced me in your favor,
   Remain the coldhearted tyrant you are!
   But your darling, whom I know you love—
   I swear by heaven that I will tear him out of
   That cruel eye of yours where he sits crowned
   Instead of me. *(to Viola)* Come with me, boy.
   My thoughts are full of mischief.
   I'll sacrifice the lamb I love *(he means Viola)*,
   To spite the raven's heart that lives
   Within a dove *(he means Olivia)*.

VIOLA: And I would willingly and happily
   Die a thousand deaths,
   If that would give you peace of mind.

*(The **duke** and **Viola** start to go.)*

84

OLIVIA: Where is Cesario going?

VIOLA: After the man I love—
   More than I love my eyes, more than my life,
   More than I shall ever love a wife.
   If I am lying, you gods above
   Punish me for tainting my love!

OLIVIA *(thinking she is being jilted)*: Alas, how I
   have been misled!

VIOLA: Who has misled you? Who does you
   wrong?

OLIVIA: Have you forgotten? Has it been so long?
   Call the holy father.

*(An **attendant** exits.)*

DUKE (to Viola): Come away!

OLIVIA: Where, my lord? Cesario, husband, stay.

DUKE: Husband?

OLIVIA: Yes, husband. Can he deny it?

DUKE *(to Viola)*: Her husband, sir?

VIOLA: No, my lord, not I!

OLIVIA: Alas, it is cowardly to deny your
   Own identity. Fear not, Cesario.
   Take possession of your good fortune.
   Be what you know you are!
   Then you are as great as him you fear.

*(The **priest** enters.)*

   Welcome, Father! Father, I ask you

To tell all you know about what
Happened between this youth and me.

PRIEST: A contract eternally binding of love,
Confirmed by holding hands, and
Proven with a holy kiss,
Strengthened by the exchange of your rings.
All the ceremony of this agreement was sealed
By me as priest and witness.
This took place only two hours ago.

DUKE *(to Viola):* Oh, you lying cub!
What will you be like by the time you're gray?
Or will your craftiness grow so fast
That you'll trip yourself up?
Farewell, then. But be sure our paths
Never cross in the future.

VIOLA: My lord, I swear—

OLIVIA: Oh, do not swear!
Keep some of your honor, despite your fear.

(Sir Andrew Aguecheek enters, his head injured.)

SIR ANDREW: For the love of God, a surgeon!
Send one to Sir Toby right away.

OLIVIA: What's the matter?

SIR ANDREW: He has split my skull and given
Sir Toby a cut head, too. Help us!
I'd give a hundred dollars to go home.

OLIVIA: Who has done this, Sir Andrew?

SIR ANDREW: The count's gentleman, that

Cesario fellow. We thought he was a coward, but he's the devil himself!

DUKE: My man Cesario?

SIR ANDREW *(noticing Viola for the first time)*: By God, here he is! *(to Viola)* You broke my head for nothing! What I did, Sir Toby made me do.

VIOLA: Why speak to me? I never hurt you. You drew your sword on me without cause, But I was polite to you and didn't hurt you.

SIR ANDREW: If a bloody head is a hurt, you have hurt me! I guess you think a bloody head is nothing!

*(**Sir Toby Belch** enters, drunk, led by **Feste**.)*

Here comes Sir Toby, limping. He'll have something to say. If he hadn't been drunk, he'd have fixed you better than he did!

DUKE: Well now, gentleman! How are you?

FESTE: Oh, he's drunk, since an hour ago. His eyes were glassy at eight this morning.

SIR TOBY *(staggering)*: Then he's a rogue and a staggering fool! I hate a drunken rogue!

OLIVIA: Take him away. Who has done this to them?

SIR ANDREW: I'll help you, Sir Toby, because our wounds can be dressed together.

OLIVIA: Get him to bed, and see to his injuries.

*(**Feste, Sir Toby,** and **Sir Andrew** exit. **Sebastian** enters.)*

SEBASTIAN: I'm sorry, madam, for hurting him.
But had he been my own brother,
I could have done no less to defend myself.
You're looking at me strangely.
I can tell I have offended you. Forgive me,
Sweet one, on the strength of the vows
We made to each other so recently.

DUKE *(totally amazed)*: One face. One voice.
One style of dress. And two persons!

SEBASTIAN *(seeing his old friend)*: Antonio!
Oh, my dear Antonio!
How agonizing the hours have been
Since losing you!

ANTONIO: Are you—Sebastian?

SEBASTIAN: Do you doubt it, Antonio?

ANTONIO: How have you divided yourself?
An apple, cut in two, is not more twin
Than these two creatures. Which is
 Sebastian?

OLIVIA: Amazing!

SEBASTIAN *(looking at Viola)*: Do I stand there?
I never had a brother . . . nor do I have
The divine gift of being here and everywhere.
I had a sister, whom the cruel sea has taken.
(to Viola) What relation are you to me?

What's your country? What's your name?
Who were your parents?

VIOLA: I'm from Messaline. Sebastian was
My father's name, and my brother's, too.
He was dressed like this when he drowned.
If spirits can take on both the body
And the clothes, you've come to frighten us.

SEBASTIAN: I am a spirit indeed—but of the
Material world into which I was born.
If you were a woman, since all else fits,
I'd shed my tears and say,
"Welcome, welcome, drowned Viola!"

VIOLA: My father had a mole upon his brow.

SEBASTIAN: And so had mine.

VIOLA: And died on my thirteenth birthday.

SEBASTIAN: The memory is vivid in my soul.
He finished his mortal life on the day
My sister and I turned thirteen.

VIOLA: If nothing prevents our happiness
But these masculine clothes I'm wearing,
Let me prove that I am Viola. Come meet
A captain in this town. My own clothes
Are at his house. Through his kind help,
I was saved, to serve this noble count.
All my life since then has been devoted
To this lady and this lord.

DUKE: Don't be alarmed—he's of noble blood.
If this is true, and it certainly seems to be,
I shall have a share in this most fortunate
Of shipwrecks. *(to Viola)* Boy, you have said
To me a thousand times that you would never
Love a woman as much as you love me.

VIOLA: And all those sayings I will swear again!

DUKE: Give me your hand,
And let me see you in your woman's clothes.

VIOLA: The captain who first brought me ashore
Has my clothes. He's under arrest over some
Legal matter which Malvolio has started.

OLIVIA: He will set him free. Fetch Malvolio here.
But, alas—I've just remembered. They say
He's mentally disturbed, poor gentleman.

*(**Feste** enters again, with a letter, followed by **Fabian**.)*

(to Feste) How is he, fellow?

FESTE: Truly, madam, he's doing as well
As any man in his situation can do.
He has written a letter to you.

OLIVIA: Open it, and read it.

FESTE *(using a weird sort of voice)***:** *By the Lord,
madam—*

OLIVIA: What, are you mad, too?

FESTE: No, madam, I'm only reading madness.
If your ladyship wants it spoken as it should
be, you must allow for a special voice.

OLIVIA: Please, read it as though you are sane.

FESTE: Yes, my lady. *(reading) By the Lord,
madam, you do me wrong, and the world
shall know it. Though you have sent me
into a dark room and put me in charge of
your drunken cousin, I am as sane as your
ladyship. I have your own letter that
persuaded me to act as I did. This will
defend me and put you to shame. Think
what you like about me. I should be more
polite, but I speak from a sense of injustice.
    —The Madly Used Malvolio*

OLIVIA: Did he write this?

FESTE: Yes, madam.

DUKE: This doesn't sound like madness.

OLIVIA: Set him free, Fabian, and bring him here.

*(**Fabian** exits.)*

My lord, I hope you'll accept me as a
Sister-in-law rather than a wife.
If you agree, the ceremonies will be
The same day, here at my house,
And at my expense.

DUKE: Madam, I happily accept your offer.
(to Viola) Your master releases you. And,
For your service to him—so unfeminine and
So far beneath your gentle upbringing—
And since you called me "master" for so long,
Here is my hand. *(Viola takes it.)*
From this time, you shall be your master's wife.

OLIVIA *(to Viola):* A sister—that's what you are!

*(**Fabian** enters again, with **Malvolio**.)*

DUKE: Is this the madman?

OLIVIA: Yes, my lord. How are you, Malvolio?

MALVOLIO: Madam, you have wronged me.
Wronged me terribly.

OLIVIA: Have I, Malvolio? Surely not.

MALVOLIO: Lady, you have. Please read this
letter. *(He hands her Maria's forgery.)*
You cannot deny this is your seal.
Well, admit it then,
And tell me, honestly, why you told me to

Come smiling and wearing yellow stockings.
Why did you tell me to frown at Sir Toby
And the servants? And why, after I did all this,
Did you have me kept in a dark house,
Visited by the priest, and made the biggest
Fool and idiot ever tricked? Tell me why.

OLIVIA: Alas, Malvolio, this is not my writing,
Though, I confess, it's very close.
Without question, it's Maria's handwriting.
And now that I think of it, it was Maria who
First told me you were mad. Then you came in
Smiling, acting as suggested in this letter.
This joke has been played on you very cleverly.
When we know who did it, you shall
Be both judge and jury in your own case.

FABIAN: Dear madam, let me speak.
May no quarrel or future brawl spoil
The pleasure of this present time, which
Has astonished me. In hope that it won't,
I confess most freely that Toby and I
Played this trick on Malvolio because
We didn't like his proud and rude manner.
Maria wrote this letter under Sir Toby's
  orders,
And he has married her in exchange.
How the trick was mischievously carried out
May cause laughter rather than desire
For revenge, especially if the grievances

On both sides are fairly weighed.

OLIVIA *(to Malvolio)*: Alas, you poor man!
How they've made a fool of you!

MALVOLIO: I'll have my revenge on all of you!

*(**Malvolio** exits.)*

OLIVIA: He has been terribly wronged.

DUKE *(to Fabian)*: Go after him! Make your
  peace.
He hasn't told us about the captain yet.
When that is sorted out, and the
  time is right,
We'll all be united in holy wedlock.
(to Olivia) Meantime, sweet sister,
We'll stay here.
(to Viola) Cesario—for so I'll call you
While you're dressed like a man—come.
(He offers her his arm.)
When in other garments you are seen,
You'll be Orsino's wife, and his heart's
  queen.

*(**All** exit.)*